For Jeanette, George and Iris
– J C

LITTLE TIGER PRESS
An imprint of Magi Publications
1 The Coda Centre, 189 Munster Road, London SW6 6AW
www.littletigerpress.com

First published in Great Britain 2007
This edition published 2008

Printed in Singapore

2 4 6 8 10 9 7 5 3 1

Ted, Bo and Diz
The First Adventure

Jason Chapman

LITTLE TIGER PRESS
London

It was a warm, sunny morning.
Ted, Bo and Diz were at the beach.

"It's a lovely day . . ." sang Ted as
he pumped up the dinghy.
   ". . . to be by the sea!" sang Diz,
shaking out the towels.

"Look," said Diz. "An iceberg!"

There, all curled up on the softly rocking bed of ice,
lay a family of polar bears and a baby seal.

One by one, they woke up.

Ted, Bo and Diz paddled gently towards them.
As Bo leaned forward to give the smallest
polar bear a flower, she could feel the coolness
of the icy boat on her face.

The little bear had never seen a flower before,
but he knew it was a beautiful thing.

Under the warm sun the bears told stories of their icy world, and the new friends played together, making snow castles on their island of ice.

Suddenly there was a dull crack.
The ice beneath Diz's feet broke off
and slipped away.
  "JUMP!" they all shouted, and Diz
jumped high and long, landing safely
with his friends . . .

Their island was melting!
"We could paddle home
in the boat," said
Daddy Polar Bear, but
it was too small for
all of them.

They sat and they
thought and they
waited as their
island got smaller . . .

and smaller.

Suddenly Ted jumped
into the boat.
"Wait here!" he said.
"I've got an idea."

"Be careful, Ted!" called Bo.
The new friends huddled together as
they watched Ted paddle far out to sea.

"Ted's coming back," said Mummy Polar Bear.
"He's coming back very fast!" said Diz.
Ted was with a family of whales!
"Hop aboard," said the biggest whale.

Ted, Bo and Diz waved goodbye as the bears and
baby seal set off on their long journey home.
    Soon the iceberg was no bigger than a pebble
on the beach. Bo picked it up and held it until
there was nothing left.

"Let's go home," said Ted sadly.
Diz looked out to sea and smiled.

"Look," he said. "Another iceberg!"